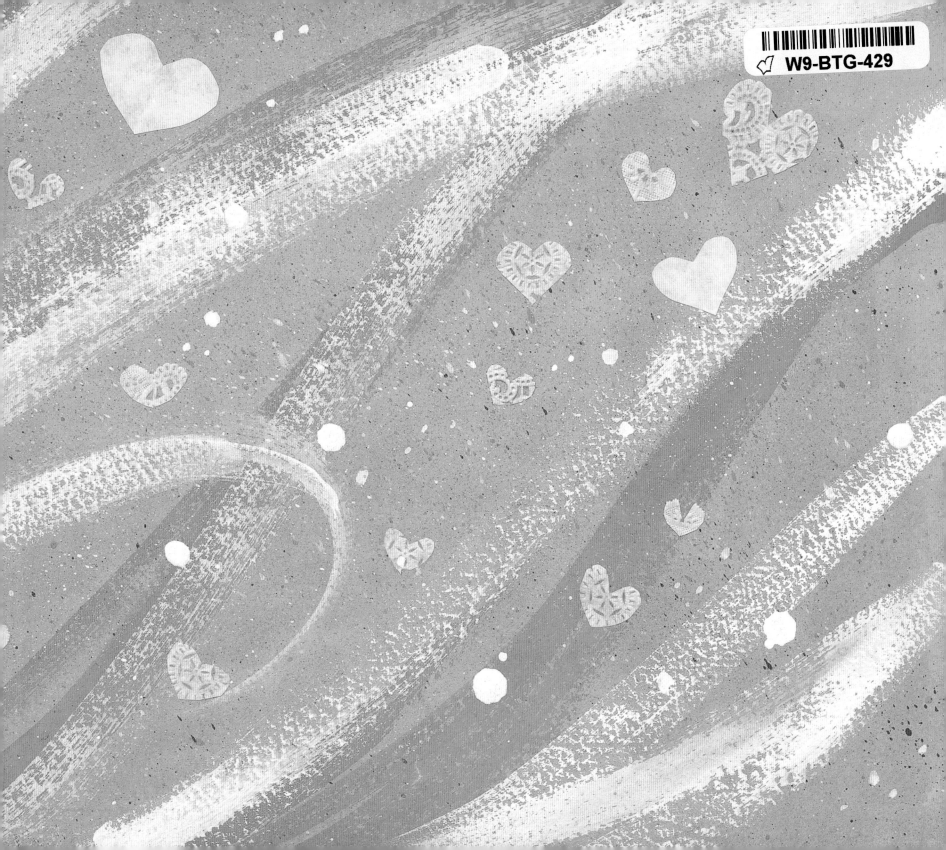

Once again, for my Valentines—
David, Becca, and Adam
—L. B. F.

To Rose and the mountains
—L. A.

Text copyright © 2010 by Laurie B. Friedman
Illustrations copyright © 2010 by Lynne Avril

Carolrhoda Books
A division of Lerner Publishing Group, Inc.
241 First Avenue North
Minneapolis, MN 55401 U.S.A.

Website address: www.lernerbooks.com

Library of Congress Cataloging-in-Publication Data

Friedman, Laurie B.
    Ruby Valentine saves the day / by Laurie Friedman ; illustrations by Lynne Avril.
       p.   cm.
    Summary: Ruby invites everyone to a grand Valentine's Day party at her mountain-
top home, but when a blizzard keeps her guests away, she decides to take the carefully
planned party into town.
    ISBN: 978-0-7613-4213-7 (lib. bdg. : alk. paper)
    [1. Stories in rhyme. 2. Valentine's Day—Fiction. 3. Parties—Fiction.
4. Blizzards—Fiction.] I. Avril, Lynne, 1951- ill. II. Title.
PZ8.3.F9116Ru 2010
[E]—dc22   2009033567

Manufactured in the United States of America
1 - DP - 7/15/10

Ruby Valentine Saves the Day

Laurie Friedman   illustrated by **Lynne Avril**

CAROLRHODA BOOKS   MINNEAPOLIS

High above the hills of Heartland,
just beyond the township sign,
with her feathered friend named Lovebird,
lived Ruby Valentine.

HEARTLAND

Now Ruby had a favorite day.
It came 'round once a year.
As she settled in to her new house,
Valentine's was drawing near.

So she decided to throw a party,
and without a moment's hesitation,
she and Lovebird sat right down
and designed the invitation.

CAUTION!
FRAGILE

HANDLE
WITH

PARTY
STUFF

*GLITTER
*GLASSES
*GLUE

PAINT

bath

Ruby mailed the invitations,
then hugged Lovebird with affection.
She told her feathered friend
they'd plan this party to perfection.

She and Lovebird hung new curtains.

They scoured every nook.

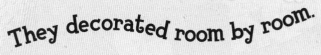
They decorated room by room.

They began to bake and cook.

When they tidied up the outside, Lovebird clung to every feather.
Ruby shivered with excitement or possibly from bad weather.

As the special
day drew closer,
Ruby counted RSVPs.
She never noticed
the thermometer.
It read 32 degrees.

"Valentine's is tomorrow, and I want everything to be just right."

Ruby tied up gifts and goody bags . . .

Then kissed Lovebird
good night.

But when Valentine's arrived,
it brought something unexpected.
Though Ruby planned out most things,
there was one thing she neglected.

"A snowstorm!" cried out Ruby.
She spent all morning on the phone.
No one could make it up the mountain.
She'd be celebrating Valentine's alone.

"My perfect party," sobbed poor Ruby. "Now it won't take place."
Lovebird wiped away the tears as they trickled down her face.

Then he looked outside the window
and said, "Do not despair!
If no one can make it here,
let's take the party there."

Ruby looked at Lovebird.
"This wasn't how I'd
planned the day."

Lovebird shook his feathers.
"There is no other way."

So, together, Ruby and Lovebird
carefully packed their sled.
As they set out down the mountain,
Ruby yelled . . .

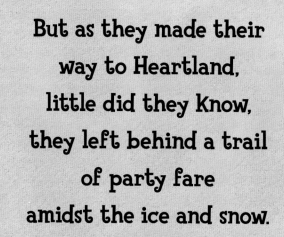

But as they made their
way to Heartland,
little did they know,
they left behind a trail
of party fare
amidst the ice and snow.

"**Happy Valentine's Day!**"
cried Ruby as she went
from door-to-door.
She gathered everyone in
Heartland from every
school and house and store.

"Time to celebrate!" smiled Ruby.
"We'll have a party in town square."

Then, horrified, she realized
her sled was dry and bare.

Ruby wrung her hands together.
"I've made a big mistake.
We can't have a party without
presents, cards, or cake."

"Nonsense!" said the townspeople.
"We'll have fun anyway.
As long as we're together,
let's enjoy the day."

So they built a giant snowman.

They sang songs around a fire.

They sounded so good together,
they formed the Heartland choir.

Everyone loved the holiday
but Ruby most of all.
It wasn't what she'd planned,
but she truly had a ball.

In the end, everyone thanked her and said, "You saved the day!"

Ruby smiled from ear to ear.
She had something she wanted to say.

"I've always loved Valentine's.
You all know that is true.
Though I celebrate every year,
today I learned something new.
Planning the day out to perfection
is not what makes it great."

"If you're with the ones you love,

that's all you need to celebrate."

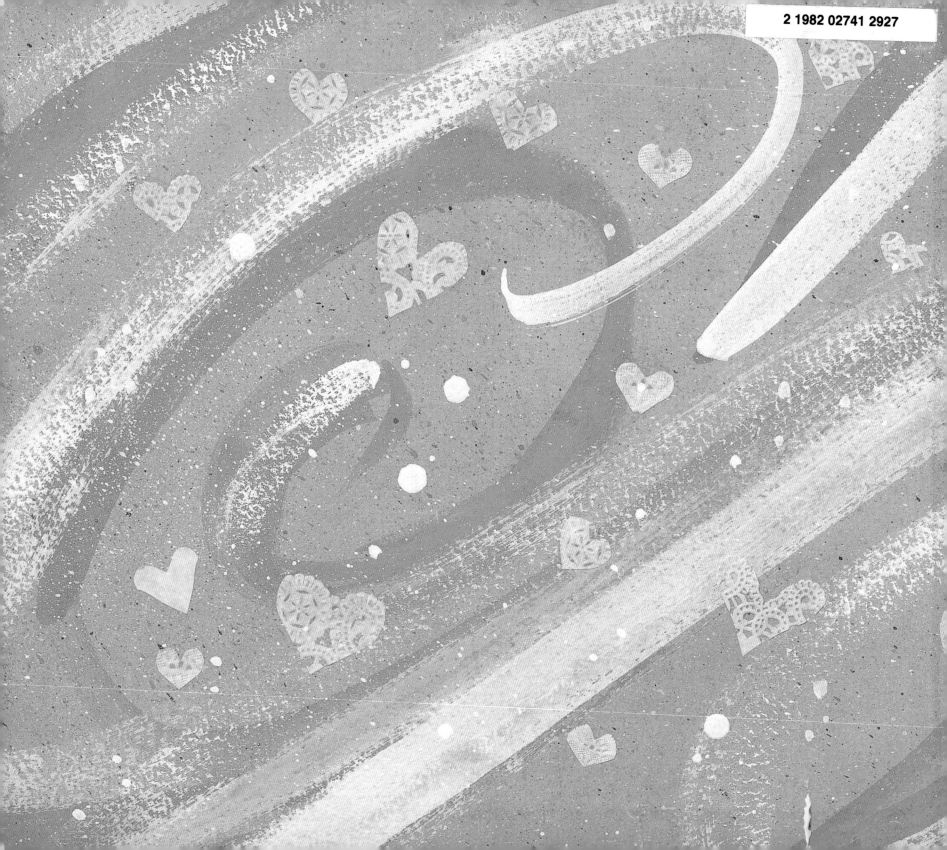